FROSTY
THE SNOW MAN

Adapted from the song of the same name

Retold by Annie North Bedford
Pictures by Corinne Malvern

GOLDEN PRESS • NEW YORK
Western Publishing Company, Inc.
Racine, Wisconsin

ABOUT FROSTY

Frosty the Snow Man was born in 1950 as the subject of a phonograph record, and soon after appeared in many different forms. A motion picture about him has been shown frequently on television, and there are Frosty toys, shirts, and games. He has been in numerous Thanksgiving Day and Christmas parades. Unlike other snow men, he is at home even in the warmest parts of the United States.

Thirty-sixth Printing, 1982

Frosty the Snow Man came to town one bright, cold winter's day.

The first real snow of the winter had fallen the night before. In the morning, out came the children, and they started to roll snowballs. Round and round the snowy yard they rolled the snowballs. Soon they had two fine big ones.

Round and round the yard again — there was a little snowball, just the right size for a snow man's head.

Billy ran home and brought two bits of coal to use for the snow man's eyes.

Sally gave him a button nose and a funny corncob pipe.
Tommy brought floppy galoshes and a scarf for the
snow man.

And Joe brought him a pair of old red mittens to wear.

"Now we need a hat," said Sally and Joe.
So they all began to look around.
Sally found an old cap. But it didn't look just right.
Billy found a battered felt hat. But it still didn't
seem right.

Just then, down the street came the whistling wind.
And it blew to their feet a shiny top hat.
  "Just what we need!" cried Sally and Joe.
  "It's like magic!" said Billy and Tommy.

It was Tommy who picked up the shiny top hat and put it on the snow man's head.

Zing! Tommy's hand sprang back with a shock.

"It *is* magic!" gasped Tommy.

"So it is," said a voice, a deep, chuckly voice they had never heard before. "And a pleasant sort of magic, if I do say so myself."

"It's the snow man!" whispered Sally.
And so it was.
"Frosty the Snow Man, at your service," said he.
That's how Frosty the Snow Man came alive.

If you have never had a snow man for a friend, you can scarcely imagine all the fun those children had.

For Frosty took them coasting — and never had their sleds slid so swiftly and so far.

Frosty helped them build a snow house — and never had blocks packed so firmly and well.

They all went ice skating — and the magical part
was that while they were with Frosty, the children
could stay out and play in the snow and never get
shivery cold.

Was it Frosty's warm heart, or his magical smile?
Whatever it was, they thought it was fine.

Each morning when the children came out to play,
Frosty had a wonderful plan all set.
  One morning he said, "Let's go shopping today.
I've never seen a store, you know."

So they all joined hands and away they skipped, off toward town where the shops stood in rows.

It was fun showing Frosty around! For he thought every window was wonderful.

All around the town they led Frosty that day, while
the warm wintry sun shone down.

Soon they came to a corner, and around the corner came a warm, gusty wind. Off went Frosty's hat. And away went Frosty after it.

Then *Tweet!* sang the traffic cop's loud whistle.
And the children could not follow Frosty, because
traffic streamed by — buses and trucks and cars.

Tweet! went the traffic cop's whistle again. The crossing stood empty before them now, but there was not a sign of Frosty to be seen.

Only his top hat rolled down the street, all by itself in the melting snow.

"Mr. Policeman!" the children cried. "Where has
Frosty the Snow Man gone?"
"Oh," said the policeman.
"Frosty the Snow Man has gone away
Where all snow men go on a sunny day.
But he'll be back at your bidding and call
Whenever great heaps of snowflakes fall."

And he will.